The Boy Who Cried
Over Everything

Betsy Childs
Illustrated by Dan Olson

Childpress CB Books

To my mother, who read to me.
—B.C.

To my mother, who sat with me
and taught me how to draw
when I was Murray's age.
—D.O.

There was once a boy named Murray. Murray was almost four years old.

Murray liked to do the things that big boys do.

He liked to shoot slingshots

and climb dirt piles

and jump over big rocks.

But one thing about Murray was not like a big boy at all. Murray cried over everything.

Oh, I don't just mean he cried when he fell down and scraped his knee. Even big boys cry at that.

No, Murray cried whenever things didn't go his way.

He cried when he found mushrooms on his pizza. (It is quite easy to pick off the mushrooms, but Murray forgot this because he was so busy crying.)

He cried when his mum put his sock on inside out. (His mum would have fixed it for him pronto, if he had asked her to. But he was too busy crying.)

He cried when his big brother Ike drank out of his Spud the Shark cup. (Ike would have given him the cup. Ike was usually kind to Murray, but sometimes Murray forgot that.)

In short, Murray cried when he was mad.
And Murray got mad a lot.

Finally, Mum and Dad had enough.
"Murray," Dad said. "You're going to have to control yourself.
You can't cry every time something doesn't go your way."

Murray thought about it. Ike hardly ever cried, even when Murray accidentally dropped Ike's favorite spitfire and broke the propeller. Murray decided he would try not to cry.

But the next time Mum handed round popsicles, she gave the last red one to the boy from across the street.

Murray squeezed his fists and furrowed his brow. He stuck out his lip. But then he remembered and decided not to cry.

Murray took a blue popsicle instead.

And when Dad took Ike to the cinema to see the new MagoMan movie, Murray didn't get to go.

He wanted to cry. But he figured if he didn't cry this time, next time they might decide he was big enough to go along.

And when they got back, they had a surprise for Murray. Dad had bought Murray his very own slingshot, just like Ike's, but red because red was Murray's favorite.

Ike helped Murray find a perfect stone. Murray was so excited about his new slingshot that he forgot the very first rule of slingshots. He didn't look before he shot. He pulled back the rubber band and let the stone fly.

And although he wasn't aiming at anything, he hit a small grey sparrow that was sitting on the branch of the pear tree.

The sparrow fell to the ground. Dad, Ike, and Murray ran over to it. Murray wanted to cry.

He did his best not to. He bit his lip and closed his eyes, but the tears would come. He wiped them away with the back of his hand.

But when he looked up from the sparrow, he saw that Ike was crying too. And when he looked at Dad, he saw that his eyes looked shiny and wet!

"Dad," Murray sniffed, "Are you crying too?"

Dad took Murray in his arms and gave him a hug.

"Yes, Murray," he said, "I'm crying too. Even big boys and big men cry when they are sad. Though it is best not to cry when you are mad, it's a good thing to cry when you're sad. I know you didn't mean to hit the bird, but I'm sad that it died."

Then Ike said, "I think we should bury the little bird!" Dad and Murray thought this was a great idea. Ike went inside to find a shoebox, while Murray helped Dad dig the hole. They covered the box with dirt and found a big rock to mark the grave.

Murray felt a lot better.

And when they went inside, Mum had a treat for them. She had bought a new box of popsicles, and every single one of them was red!

The End

Made in the USA
Lexington, KY
19 October 2014